Brittany
the Basketball
Fairy

Special thanks to
Narinder Dhami

ISBN 978-0-545-20255-8

Copyright © 2008 by Rainbow Magic Limited.

Previously published as *Naomi the Netball Fairy* by Orchard U.K. in 2008.

All rights reserved. Published by Scholastic Inc., 557 Broadway, New York, NY 10012, by arrangement with Rainbow Magic Limited.

12 11 10   18 19/0

Printed in the U.S.A.   40

First Scholastic Printing, April 2010

Brittany

the Basketball Fairy

by Daisy Meadows

LITTLE APPLE

SCHOLASTIC INC.

New York   Toronto   London   Auckland
Sydney   Mexico City   New Delhi   Hong Kong

The Fairyland Palace

Fairyl...

Parking Lot

Buses

Riding Stables

Cooke Soccer Stadium

Basketball Courts

Soccer Fields

Tippington Town

REC CENTER

Swimming Pool

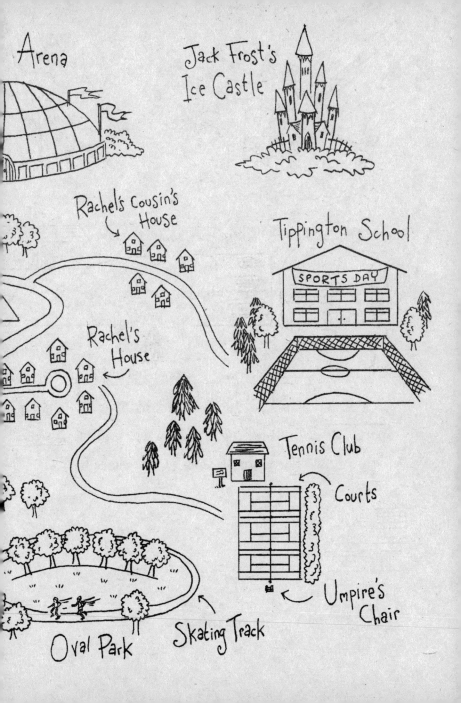

The Fairyland Olympics are about to start,
And my crafty goblins will take part.
We'll win this year, for I have a cunning plan.
I'll send my goblins to compete in Fairyland.

The magic objects that make sports safe and fun
Will be stolen by my goblins, to keep until we've won.
Sports Fairies, prepare to lose and to watch us win.
Goblins, follow my commands, and let the games begin!

Contents

Spring into Sports

"What should we do after lunch, Kirsty?"
Rachel Walker asked as she finished
her apple.

Kirsty Tate, Rachel's best friend,
grinned. "You know what I'd really
like to do?" she replied. "I'd like to find
Brittany the Basketball Fairy's magic
basketball!"

Rachel and Kirsty shared a very special secret. While vacationing on Rainspell Island, the two girls had become friends with the fairies! Now Rachel and Kirsty always helped out whenever there was a problem in Fairyland.

"Remember what Queen Titania said," Rachel reminded Kirsty. "We have to let the magic come to us."

"I know, but I'm feeling really impatient today," Kirsty replied. "If we don't find all the magic objects before I go home in a few days, Jack Frost and his goblins will win the Fairyland Olympic Cup!"

The Fairyland Olympics were starting at the end of the week, but mean Jack Frost had stolen the Sports Fairies' seven magic objects. These magical objects made sure that sports were fun and exciting, and also played fairly, in both Fairyland and the human world. But Jack Frost wanted his goblins to use the magic objects to cheat, so they would win every event of the Fairyland Olympics. He had sent the goblins into the human world, to keep the magic objects hidden, and to practice their sports. But Rachel and Kirsty had promised the Sports Fairies that they would try to get the seven objects back before the fairy games began.

Rachel sighed. "The missing objects mean that sports in our world are affected, too," she added. "I wonder how many basketball games are going wrong right now because Brittany's magic basketball is missing!"

"Well, we've already found Helena's riding helmet, Stacey's soccer ball, and Zoe's skate lace," Kirsty pointed out.

Rachel nodded. "We can't let Jack Frost and his goblins win the cup by cheating," she said seriously. "Especially since King Oberon told us that the cup is filled with good luck. Imagine all the trouble the goblins could cause with lots of luck to help them!"

Just then, Rachel's mom came into the kitchen. "Girls, have you finished your lunch?" Mrs. Walker asked. "I don't know if you've decided what you want to do this afternoon, but I thought this might be fun." She put a brochure down on the table.

"*Spring into Sports!*" Rachel read aloud. "*Come and try a new sport at Tippington Rec Center on Tuesday—absolutely free!*"

Kirsty opened the brochure. "Look!" she exclaimed. "Bowling, badminton, croquet, baseball, and basketball . . ." Kirsty glanced meaningfully at Rachel.

The Sports Fairies had told the girls that the goblins who had one of the magic objects would be extremely attracted to that sport, especially since the goblins wanted to practice for the Fairyland Olympics. So Rachel and Kirsty knew it was possible that the goblin with the magic basketball might show up at the rec center.

"Why don't you go and play a couple of sports?" Rachel's mom suggested, clearing away the plates.

"Good idea, Mom," said Rachel, jumping up from the table.

"It does sound like fun," Kirsty agreed.

The girls pulled on their sneakers and headed into the village. The rec center was just off of High Street. There were fields for football and soccer in front

of the building, and games were taking
place on all of them. There were even
groups of people standing around, waiting
for a turn.

"Looks like we're not the only ones
who want to 'Spring into Sports!'" Kirsty
said as they headed toward the glass
doors. "Do you think the goblins might
be here?"

Rachel nodded. "Maybe, but if they

are, it's going to be hard to spot them with so many people around."

The girls went inside the rec center and watched a badminton match. Then they peeked into the yoga studio, where a class was taking place.

"Let's go check out the basketball courts," Rachel suggested, as they passed the gym. "They're outside, near the running track."

When the girls arrived, they found

that there were games in progress on all of the basketball courts except for one. Two teams were stretching next to the empty court, ready to start a game.

"Everything looks normal," Kirsty said quietly. "I don't see any goblins."

"Neither do I," Rachel agreed. Then she noticed a girl hurrying toward them. "Kirsty, that's my friend Abby, from school!" Rachel exclaimed. She waved at the girl as she rushed past. "Hey, Abby!"

Abby stopped, looking nervous. "Oh, hi, Rachel," she said. "Sorry, I'm in such a hurry that I didn't notice you there! Is this your friend Kirsty?"

Rachel nodded.

"Hi, Abby," said Kirsty. "Is there something wrong? You look kind of worried."

"Oh, everything's going wrong today!" Abby replied, heaving a huge sigh. "I'm on a basketball team with my friends, and we were just challenged to a game by some boys who call themselves 'The Mean Green Basketball Team.'"

"The Mean Green Basketball Team?" Rachel repeated. "What a crazy name!"

"Yes—and they *are* mean!" Abby told her. "They've already easily beaten all the other teams and they acted kind of strange about it. They painted their hands with green paint, and they're wearing green masks." She shook her head.

"They're really taking the team name seriously!"

Kirsty felt a shiver of excitement run down her spine. She glanced at Rachel and could see that her friend was thinking exactly the same thing: Could The Mean Green Basketball Team be a group of goblins?

Rachel and Kirsty Join the Team

Abby bit her lip nervously. "The problem is," she went on, "two of our players haven't shown up. The game is starting in a few minutes, and we don't even have a full roster! I was just on my way into the rec center to see if I could find some people to help us out. Each team is supposed to have seven players. Five play at a time, and two others rotate in."

Rachel glanced at Kirsty again. She knew they needed to find out if the green players were goblins, and this was their chance!

"Kirsty and I could play for your team," Rachel offered. "Couldn't we, Kirsty?"

Kirsty nodded as a smile brightened Abby's face.

"Oh, you'd do that?" Abby said, eagerly. "That would be great!"

"But we don't have uniforms," Kirsty said, glancing at the warm-up pants she and Rachel were wearing.

"Don't worry about that," Abby told her, leading the girls toward the court. "No one does! It's a practice session, not a real game. I can get you some extra pinnies."

"OK," said Kirsty. "But I'd better warn you, I'm not very good at basketball."

Abby smiled. "Don't worry. No one's playing very well today except The

Mean Green Basketball Team," she confessed. "Everyone seems to have butterfingers and two left feet, even me."

Rachel looked sympathetic. She and Kirsty both knew why everyone was being clumsy. It was because Brittany's magic basketball was missing.

"Well, we'll do our best," Rachel declared in a determined voice, and Kirsty nodded.

"Rachel, I've seen you playing basketball at school, and I know you're good at shooting," Abby said as they reached the court. "So you can be our secret weapon!"

Rachel blushed. "I'll try to get a couple of baskets," she promised.

Abby found two pinnies on the side

of the court and handed them to
Rachel and Kirsty.

"Rachel, you can
play center. Kirsty,
you'll be a forward,"
she explained as they
ran onto the court.
"You can mostly play
defense. Now come and
meet the rest of the team."

Abby took Rachel and Kirsty over
to a small group of girls, who were
standing at one end of the court. They
all looked nervous.

"Cheer up, everyone!" Abby
exclaimed. "I found two more players!"

The rest of the team brightened up
immediately.

"That's great!" said a tall girl with

fair hair. "We're going to need a full team. The Mean Green Basketball Team players are really good!"

Rachel and Kirsty looked over at The Mean Green Basketball Team. The players were practicing their handling skills at the other end of the court. The team members wore caps to hide their faces and were passing

the ball quickly and confidently to one another.

"They're definitely goblins, Kirsty," Rachel whispered, catching a glimpse of a pointy green nose under one of the caps.

"I know," Kirsty agreed quietly. "And look at that goblin spinning the basketball on his finger over there."

Rachel stared at the goblin and gasped. A faint shimmer of purple sparkles surrounded the ball spinning on his finger! "It's Brittany's magic basketball!" Rachel exclaimed in a low voice.

"Yes! Now all we have to do is get it back," Kirsty pointed out.

"Let's get started," called the referee, blowing her whistle. "We'll scrimmage for just fifteen minutes today." She flipped a coin in the air and turned to the biggest goblin, who was the captain.

"Heads!" called the captain.

20

The referee examined the coin. "Heads it is," she announced. "The Mean Green Basketball Team will start the game."

The goblins quickly dashed into their positions. The referee blew her whistle. Immediately, the goblin in the center passed the magic basketball to the goblin on his right. Kirsty and another player moved to guard him, but the second goblin threw the ball high over their heads and straight to one of his teammates. In an instant, the ball swished cleanly through the hoop.

"Two-zero," called the referee as the goblins whooped with glee and gave each other high fives.

Dismayed, Kirsty glanced down the court at Rachel. The goblins were ahead, and no one on their team had even touched the ball yet!

Abby inbounded the ball, but one of the goblins dashed in front of Kirsty and stole it away. Once again, the goblins were in control. After a series of amazing passes, the goblin center sidestepped Kirsty and tossed the ball through the hoop again.

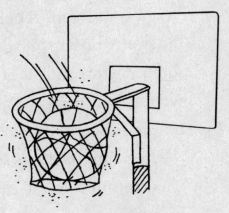

"Four-zero!" the referee shouted.

Rachel watched helplessly as the goblins dribbled the ball swiftly and smoothly and scored lots of baskets. The goblins were too quick for the players on Abby's team. Rachel realized that this meant the human players weren't benefiting from the magic of Brittany's basketball. The girls didn't have the ball long enough for the magic to rub off, because the sneaky goblins were always stealing it away! Rachel looked across the court at Kirsty and shook her head sadly. At this rate, Rachel realized, they were never going to get Brittany's magic basketball back!

Then one of the goblins tried to lob the ball high up into the air toward one of his teammates, but Abby jumped up and actually managed to intercept it.

"Abby!" Rachel shouted eagerly, waving her arms. "Over here!"

Abby passed the ball toward Rachel, but just as Rachel was about to catch it, a goblin leaped in front of her and swatted the ball away.

"Oh no!" Rachel sighed. She stood beneath the basket, watching sadly as a goblin dribbled the ball speedily down to the other end of the court. As she stood there, a shower of purple sparkles rained down around her. Rachel glanced up in surprise. Brittany the Basketball Fairy was sitting on the rim of the hoop!

Fairy Help at Hand

Brittany waved at Rachel and fluttered
down to join her. She wore a blue-and-
purple sports skirt and shirt, and matching
basketball shoes. Her blond hair was
neatly tied up with ribbons and a purple
headband.

"Don't be sad, Rachel," Brittany
whispered, landing lightly on Rachel's
shoulder. "I'm sure we'll find another

way to get my basketball back."

"I hope so," Rachel said eagerly. "It's great to see you, Brittany!"

The fairy grinned and slipped quickly into the pocket of Rachel's warm-up pants.

At that moment, the referee blew her whistle. "The Mean Green Basketball Team wins, twenty to zero!" she announced.

The goblins cheered loudly. Meanwhile, Abby's team trudged away.

"What a blowout!" Abby groaned, as she and Kirsty came over to Rachel. "We hardly touched the ball the entire game. But thanks for playing with us, you guys. We're going to try some of the other sports now. Do you want to come?"

"Thanks, but I think I'll look around a little more first," Rachel said. "We'll find you later."

As Abby waved good-bye, Rachel pulled Kirsty to the side of the court. She wanted to get away from the goblins, who were still celebrating.

"Look who's here," Rachel whispered.

"Hello, Kirsty," called Brittany, fluttering out of Rachel's pocket.

"Oh, Brittany!" Kirsty exclaimed. "Thank goodness you're here. We really need your help to get the magic basketball."

Brittany pointed her wand at the giddy goblins. "We'd better stay close to

them, and wait for our chance to grab the ball," she suggested. "Look, they're leaving."

Two other teams had shown up for a game, and the goblins were hurrying off the court, still chatting excitedly. Their captain led the way, carrying the magic basketball.

Brittany ducked back into Rachel's pocket, and the girls followed the goblins. They were careful to stay a short distance behind the goblins, so that they wouldn't be seen.

"Okay, we're going to practice shooting now," the captain said bossily. He led his team into the rec center. "We'll use one of the indoor courts where it's nice and quiet."

The other goblins groaned.

"That's boring!" one complained loudly. "Can't we do something else? We're great at shooting already!"

The captain glared at him. "What do you mean, *boring*?" he snapped. "There's always room for improvement. Now, come on!"

He marched onto one of the indoor
courts. The other goblins trailed
after him, grumbling to one another.

Kirsty, Rachel, and Brittany peeked
through the open doors as the goblins
began shooting at one of the hoops with
the magic basketball.

"They're scoring almost every time,"
Rachel whispered. "Even from three-
point range!"

The goblins were so confident that they began doing silly tricks. They tried turning their backs to the hoop and shooting over their shoulders or from between their legs. Sometimes they missed, but most of the time they still managed to make basket after basket.

Brittany sniffed as the ball swooshed through the hoop yet again. "It's my magic basketball that's doing all the work," she said angrily. "Those goblins wouldn't be any good without it."

"Oh!" Kirsty gasped suddenly. "Brittany, you've given me an idea. I think I know how we can get your magic basketball back!"

"What do we have to do, Kirsty?"
Rachel asked.

"Brittany, can you use your wand to
make a new basketball?" Kirsty asked.
"One that sparkles like it's magic?"

Brittany nodded. "Sure," she replied.
"But it won't really have magical
powers. It'll just be an ordinary
basketball."

"That's okay," Kirsty replied. "But can you also use your magic to make the goblins' hoop repel any basketball that's thrown at it?"

This time, Brittany frowned. "I can do that with a simple wave of my wand," she said slowly. "But the spell won't last for very long because my magic basketball is so powerful. It will eventually overcome any repelling magic I put on the hoop."

"Well, my plan shouldn't take too long to start working," said Kirsty. "We just need to convince the goblins that the real magic basketball isn't very magical anymore, and that we have a new, improved basketball that's full of magic! Then they might trade with us."

Rachel looked confused. "But the goblins will only want our ball if they see us scoring lots of baskets with it," she pointed out.

"Exactly," Kirsty agreed.

"But how is that going to work?" Rachel asked, looking even more puzzled. "Brittany just said that the other basketball won't really be magic at all. And the goblins

will only believe it's magical if it goes in the hoop every time!"

Kirsty grinned at her. "That's where you come in, Rachel," she explained. "You'll have to use your fabulous shooting skills to persuade the goblins that we really do have a magic basketball!"

Rachel gulped. "You mean I have to get the ball through the hoop every time?"

"That's the plan," Kirsty replied.
"Do you think you can do it, Rachel?"

"I don't know." Rachel looked a little
anxious. "I probably won't be very good
at shooting today because the magic
basketball isn't in its proper place."

"But it *is* in the same room," Brittany
said. "So some of its magic will help
you."

"OK," Rachel agreed. "I'll just
concentrate and try my best to make
a basket every time the
goblins are looking. It'll
be hard, but it's not
impossible."

"Go, Rachel!"
Brittany cheered,
twirling around with
excitement. "Here's

your new basketball." She raised her wand and made a circle of purple sparkles in midair. Then the sparkles transformed into a basketball that

shimmered slightly, just like the magic one. The ball floated toward Rachel, and she easily caught it.

The goblins had been taking turns shooting free throws, but now they were arguing about who was next.

"It's my turn!" the smallest goblin screeched, trying to grab the ball from the captain.

"I'm in charge," the captain growled. "I'll decide who's next!"

"I think it's time someone else had a chance to be captain," another goblin declared.

"No way!" the captain yelled.

As the goblins argued furiously,
Brittany grinned at Rachel and Kirsty.
"Now I can put the repelling spell on the
hoop while the goblins aren't looking,"
she whispered.

Brittany pointed her wand at the
goblins' hoop, and a rush of purple
sparkles streamed through the air.
Rachel and Kirsty watched as the

sparkles circled the hoop and quickly began to fade.

Just then, a tall, thin goblin looked up. "Hey!" he shouted, staring at the faint glitter around the hoop. "What's that? It looks like fairy magic."

Rachel, Kirsty, and Brittany stared at each other in dismay. Had their plan failed already?

Girls Go into Action

The goblins all stared up at the hoop, but the last few sparkles had already vanished.

"What are you talking about?" the captain snapped. "There's nothing there!"

"You're seeing things!" another goblin teased, and they all burst out laughing.

"But I *did* see some sparkles," the tall goblin insisted. He rushed forward and

stared up at the hoop, while the other
goblins waited impatiently.

"OK, I can't see any fairies," the
tall goblin mumbled finally, looking
embarrassed.

"Your shot," the captain ordered,
shoving the ball into the goblin's arms.

The goblin squinted
at the hoop and then
threw the magic
basketball toward
it. The ball curved
toward the hoop in
a perfect arc. But,
as the ball dropped,
it missed the hoop
completely.

"What's happening?" the tall goblin
complained, looking confused as the ball
fell to the ground.

"You're useless, that's what's
happening!" another goblin said rudely.
He grabbed the basketball and launched
a shot himself. But the ball missed again,
even though it looked as if it was aimed
right at the basket.

"The goblins are starting to look worried," Brittany whispered to the girls as the captain took a shot and missed. "I think it's time for you to do your thing, Rachel."

Rachel, Kirsty, and Brittany came out from their hiding place behind the doors to the basketball court. They hurried to the hoop at the empty end of the court. Rachel had the new basketball tucked under her arm.

The goblins didn't notice them—they were too busy arguing about why the magic basketball didn't seem to be working anymore.

"Here goes," Rachel murmured, positioning herself in front of the hoop and carefully taking a shot. The ball rose smoothly and fell cleanly through the hoop.

"Nice job, Rachel!" Brittany and Kirsty cheered, applauding loudly.

Feeling more confident, Rachel tried again. This time, the ball trembled on the rim of the hoop, but it still went in.

As Kirsty and Brittany clapped, Kirsty
glanced over her shoulder. The goblins
were staring at them from the other
end of the court.

"The goblins don't look very happy,"
Kirsty whispered.

Rachel grinned and immediately
made another perfect basket.

This was too much for the goblins!

They all came rushing over. One of
them was carrying Brittany's magic
basketball under his arm.

"How come you're making all your
baskets and we're not?" the captain
demanded.

"Oh, it's because I have this
wonderful magic basketball," Rachel
simply replied, holding the ball up.

"But *we* have the magic basketball!" one of the goblins said, puzzled.

Brittany looked at their basketball. "Oh, you've got the old magic basketball," she told the goblins. "This is the brand-new, super-magic basketball!"

Rachel took another shot. The goblins all muttered jealously to one another as

they watched the ball swish through the hoop once again.

"The new magic basketball is better than the old one!" the captain declared.

"Yes, give us the new basketball!" the goblins begged eagerly. One of them even began sneaking up on Rachel.

Brittany frowned. "If you try to steal the magic basketball, I'll turn Rachel and Kirsty into fairies and we'll all fly away," she told the sneaky goblin, lifting her wand. "Then you'll *never* get the new basketball!"

The goblins looked at each other and frowned.

"Well, can we just try the new magic

basketball?" the small goblin whined. "Please?"

Brittany looked thoughtful for a moment. "Well," the fairy said reluctantly, "we'll trade our new basketball for your old one if you agree to go back to Goblin Grotto immediately."

"Done!" the goblin with the ball agreed eagerly, holding it out toward Rachel. But just as she was about to take it . . .

"STOP!" yelled the
captain in a
suspicious voice.
The goblin
snatched the
ball out of
Rachel's grasp.
She glanced
anxiously at
Kirsty and
Brittany. Had
the captain
guessed what
was going on?
"Why do you
want us to go
back to Goblin Grotto?"
the captain demanded.
Brittany put her hands on her hips.

"Because if you stay in the human world much longer, someone's going to realize you're goblins!" the fairy replied quickly. "Your caps and tracksuits aren't very good disguises. And you know we can't let humans find out about Fairyland and Goblin Grotto."

The captain nodded thoughtfully. "That's true," he muttered. "OK, let's make the switch!"

The goblin held out Brittany's basketball again, but before Rachel could take it, the captain leaped forward again.

"STOP!" he shouted.

"Oh, make up your mind," the goblin grumbled, yanking the ball away from Rachel once again.

"We agree to the trade on one condition," the captain declared. He pointed at Kirsty. "She hasn't tried shooting. I want to make sure the new magic basketball works on everyone. Let's see her make a basket!"

"Me?" Kirsty gulped. She'd never made a basket in her life!

"You can do it, Kirsty," Rachel whispered encouragingly, handing her the ball.

Brittany fluttered over to Kirsty. "Take a deep breath and steady yourself," she told her quietly. "Keep your eye on the hoop, and make your shot as smooth as possible. Most important, believe in yourself."

Kirsty nodded, feeling very nervous. Her palms were sweating as she held the ball up and looked at the hoop. She tried to remember exactly how Rachel had made all her amazing baskets.

After a moment, Kirsty took her shot. The ball flew through the air, and Rachel, Brittany, and Kirsty all gasped as it bounced off the backboard and rattled around the rim. Would the ball go through the hoop or not?

A Beautiful Basket

It seemed to take forever, but the ball finally dropped through the hoop. Kirsty almost burst with relief as she grinned delightedly at Rachel and Brittany.

"OK, we definitely want that magic basketball," the goblin captain decided quickly.

Kirsty picked up the ball and traded with the goblin who had Brittany's magic basketball. "Now, remember, you're going straight home to Goblin Grotto," Brittany reminded them.

"Yeah! We can show the new magic basketball to Jack Frost," the goblin with the ball exclaimed. "He's going to be so happy with us!"

"Give me the ball," the captain ordered.

"No!" the goblin answered rudely, running off across the court. The other goblins chased after him, and Rachel, Kirsty, and Brittany laughed.

"They're going to be disappointed
when they find out that the new magic
basketball isn't actually magical at all,"
said Rachel.

"Oh, but it is!" Brittany replied
with a wink. "We didn't lie. The new
ball is magical because it *is* made
of fairy magic. It just doesn't make
anyone good at basketball, that's
all!" She grinned, flew over to Kirsty,
and took the magic basketball. As

Brittany touched it, the ball shrank to its Fairyland size. Then Brittany tapped the ball with her wand, making it sparkle even more brightly for a moment.

"Thank you, girls!" she cried. "Basketball games everywhere will be fun and fair again. Now, I need to return to Fairyland and tell the other Sports Fairies the good news." She smiled at Rachel and Kirsty as she spun the magic basketball around on one finger. "Keep up the good work." And Brittany flew out the door, leaving a trail of dazzling purple sparkles behind her.

"Well, you were right, Rachel," Kirsty said happily as they went off to search for Abby and her friends. "The magic *did* come to us!"

"Now we're going to have fun trying out other sports." Rachel laughed. "And hopefully we'll have more exciting adventures with the Sports Fairies, too!"

RAINBOW magic™

THE SPORTS FAIRIES

Now Rachel and Kirsty need to help

Samantha
the Swimming Fairy!

Jack Frost's goblins stole Samantha's
magic goggles. Can Rachel and Kirsty
help Samantha outsmart the goblins
and get the goggles back?

Join their next adventure
in this special sneak peek!

Swimming Pool Puzzle

"Fetch, Buttons!" Rachel Walker called, throwing her dog's favorite ball across the yard.

Kirsty Tate, Rachel's best friend, who was staying with the Walkers for spring break, smiled. "Buttons loves exercise, doesn't he?" she said, as the dog bounded after the ball.

"And we're almost as fit as he is. We've had such an athletic week!"

Rachel grinned. Without her parents knowing, Rachel and Kirsty had been taking part in a new fairy adventure this week. They were helping the Sports Fairies track down their missing magic objects. Rachel felt as if she and Kirsty were the luckiest girls in the world, being friends with the fairies.

"Good dog!" said Rachel's dad, coming out to the yard with Mrs. Walker. Buttons rushed back with the ball in his mouth, then dropped it at Rachel's feet and went to his water bowl to drink thirstily.

"Phew, it's hot," Mrs. Walker said, fanning herself. "It's the perfect day for a swim."

Rachel and Kirsty looked at each other excitedly. Swimming would be a great idea—especially since Samantha the Swimming Fairy's magic goggles were still missing.

"Ooh, yes, can we go swimming?" Rachel asked.

"The Tippington pool is closed," Mr. Walker pointed out, "so you'd have to go to Aqua World in the next town over." Then he frowned. "But I took the car into the garage to be serviced, so I won't be able to drive you there."

"You could take the bus," Mrs. Walker said. "The 41 goes all the way there. If you take your cell phone, Rachel, you can let me know when you'll be back."

"Hooray!" cheered Rachel and Kirsty together. They both rushed inside to pack their swimming things. Then Rachel's mom walked them to the bus stop. . . .

RAINBOW magic™

THE PET FAIRIES

When a pet finds a home, it's magical!

www.scholastic.com
www.rainbowmagiconline.com

HiT entertainment

PET

RAINBOW magic™

SPECIAL EDITION

Three Books in One!
More Rainbow Magic Fun!

■SCHOLASTIC
www.scholastic.com
www.rainbowmagiconline.com

HIT entertainment

RMSPECIAL2

RAINBOW magic™

There's Magic in Every Series!

The Rainbow Fairies

The Weather Fairies

The Jewel Fairies

The Pet Fairies

The Fun Day Fairies

The Petal Fairies

The Dance Fairies

The Music Fairies

The Sports Fairies

The Party Fairies

Read them all!

◼ SCHOLASTIC

www.scholastic.com
www.rainbowmagiconline.com

RMFAIRY2